Veil of Perception
Sixteen Psychological Mind-Benders

"Delve into the shadows of the mind, where twisted tales of suspense await, unravelling the delicate threads of sanity and gripping your every thought. Brace yourself for a journey into the heart of psychological thrillers."

Yashvardhan Jha

For
M.K.Jha And P.Jha
(my parents)
And my friends

Chapter 1: "The Enigmatic Sanctuary: A Haunting Hotel Mystery"

The Shining Hotel, with its gothic architecture casting lengthy shadows across the barren terrain, loomed **menacingly** on the storm-lashed cliffside. Dr. Yash, a renowned detective who spent half of his life fighting in World War 2, was sent to the hotel to look into the patient Siya Sharma's abrupt disappearance.

Dr. Yash, plagued by dreams and his own demons, couldn't shake the **déjà vu** sense as he entered the opulent lobby of The Shining Hotel. Mr. Dheeraj, the mysterious **proprietor**, who emanated an air of mystery and authority, greeted him.

Assigned to Room 237, Dr. Yash began his investigation. The Hotel was said to have a dark past, harbouring visitors with unusual ailments. Instead of mental illness, the guests were supposed to suffer from a variety of anomalies, including **phantasmagoric delusions**, reality disintegration, and ethereal obsessions.

Dr. Yash had strange **hallucinations** and unnerving experiences as he investigated the case further. Screams and whispers filled the corridors, and the portraits on the walls seemed to stare at him with terrifying eyes. He began to doubt the veracity of his surroundings as well as his own sanity.

Dr. Yash introduced himself to the remaining guests, each of whom had an enigmatic presence. Ms. Shreya, who believed she could speak with the spirits of the deceased, and Mr. Sagnik, an artist whose paintings seemed to contain more than what greeted the eye, were among those present. The hotel staff's foreboding stillness and mysterious smiles contributed to the eerie atmosphere.

Dr. Yash explored the depths of The Shining Hotel, uncovering its dark secrets, driven by his quest to find Siya. He discovered a secret basement full of old journals chronicling the hotel's previous macabre experiments on its visitors. The distinction between the living and the dead got increasingly hazy.

Dr. Yash's health began to deteriorate after watching the unusual behaviour of the guests and employees. Something seemed strange and off about this establishment, and the vibe was really negative. When he met Ms Shreya, she urged him to leave this place as soon as possible or else he would die since his head was filled with screams and haunting from his past experiences from World War II.

Dr. Yash's nightmares became more intense as the chaos and confusion increased, combining with his waking existence. Memories

emerged, showing that he had previously been a patient at the Shining Hotel. His perspective of reality was broken by the truth of his background, prompting him to doubt the nature of the hotel, its guests, and his own identity.

The truth was revealed in a climactic encounter with Mr. Dheeraj. The Shining Hotel was more than just a shelter for disturbed visitors; it was a laboratory where identities were shattered and minds were manipulated. Dr. Yash was a patient caught in a web of deception and reprogrammed memories, not an investigator.

The realisation sent shockwaves through Dr. Yash's consciousness. As he succumbed to the dark forces that enveloped the Shining Hotel, the line between patient and doctor, perpetrator and victim, dissolved. The once-determined detective found himself lost within the labyrinth of his own mind, forever imprisoned within the confines of the enigmatic hotel.

The legend of the Shining Hotel lives on, whispered in hushed tones by those who dare to speak its name. Its secrets remain locked away, and those who venture too close risk losing their grasp on reality, forever trapped in the depths of their own shattered minds.

WORD MEANINGS

1. **Menacingly**: in a way that makes you think that someone is going to do something bad or that something bad is going to happen

   Eg: She glared menacingly at him.

2. **Déjà vu:** the strange feeling that in some way you have already experienced what is happening now

   Eg: *When I met her, I had a strange feeling of déjà vu.*

3. **Proprietor:** a person who owns a particular type of business, especially a hotel, a shop, or a company that makes newspapers.

4. **Phantasmagoric:** full of different images, like something in a confused dream.

5. **Delusions:** belief in something that is not true.

6. **Hallucinations:** an experience in which you see, hear, feel, or smell something that does not exist, usually because you are ill or have taken a drug.

Chapter 2: "Eternal Conundrum"

The island remained firm in the middle of the huge ocean, its frightening presence luring those who dared to venture into its depths. It was a place cloaked in mystery and strange whispers. Lavanya, a young woman seeking adventure, was pulled to the island's intriguing charm, ignorant of the difficulties that awaited her.

Boarding a ferry boat with a group of fellow thrill-seekers, Lavanya embarked on an excursion that promised excitement and discovery. The journey was uneventful until an unexpected storm materialised, engulfing the boat in a relentless tempest. Waves crashed against the vessel, and panic filled the air as it was swept off course.

When the tempest finally subsided, Lavanya and her companions found themselves marooned on a deserted island. They soon

discovered a peculiar structure—an ancient lighthouse, standing tall amidst the desolate landscape. Seeking refuge, they sought solace within its walls, unaware of the enigmatic force that resided within.

As night fell, strange occurrences began to unfold. Whispers echoed through the halls, carrying secrets from forgotten times. The lighthouse seemed to defy logic, its corridors twisting and turning in impossible ways. Doors led to different places with each passage, confounding their attempts to escape.

As Lavanya and her companions explored further, they encountered other individuals who claimed to have been stranded on the island for years. These survivors were caught in an unending cycle of despair and confusion, forever trapped within the **labyrinthine** confines of the lighthouse.

Memories grew fragmented with each repeat of the cycle, and time became an unintelligible concept. Lavanya tried to keep her sanity, piecing together parts of her background and the island's true nature. She found that the lighthouse had a dark secret—an ancient entity that thrived on the desperation and uncertainty of those unlucky enough to be caught in its clutches.

Driven by her determination to break the cycle, Lavanya formed an alliance with a fellow survivor named Yash, who possessed a deep understanding of the island's mechanics. Together, they **deciphered** the patterns and illusions that bound them, gradually unravelling the island's enigma.

Their escape route took them through **perilous** challenges and encounters with supernatural beings. The island appeared to be an interdimensional node where time and space merged, defying conventional reasoning. Lavanya and Yash deciphered the island's riddles, confronting the malignant entity that tried to imprison them forever.

Lavanya and Yash battled the ancient thing in a climactic battle of wills, opposing its manipulations and exploiting its flaws. Their perseverance and resilience interrupted the pattern, destroying the island's grip and allowing them to flee. **Could they, however?**

As they emerged from the lighthouse, the island faded into the distance, its dark secrets sealed away once more. Lavanya and Yash, forever marked by their harrowing experience, emerged stronger and wiser. Their shared ordeal forged an unbreakable bond, a testament to the indomitable nature of the human spirit.

They were unaware that they were caught in a never-ending time loop from which they could not break free. When they realise they are trapped, their smiling faces and feelings of relief will soon fade.

"Eternal Conundrum" serves as a cautionary tale, reminding us of the fragile nature of our perception and the inherent mysteries of the world around us. It urges us to question our reality and embrace the unknown, for it is through our unyielding pursuit of truth that we transcend the boundaries of the ordinary and embark on extraordinary journeys of self-discovery.

WORD MEANINGS

1. **Labyrinthine:** used to describe something that has a lot of parts and is therefore confusing

   Eg: Beneath the city lies a labyrinthine network of tunnels.

2. **Deciphered:** to discover the meaning of something written badly or in a difficult or hidden way

3. **Perilous:** extremely dangerous

Chapter 3:"Fragments of Fate"

Madhuban, once a vibrant and busy metropolis, was now covered in dense fog, cut off from the rest of the world. The Desi Dhaba Hotel, an ancient and enigmatic guest house rumoured to harbour a terrible secret, lay in the centre of this spooky town. During a stormy night, as lightning ripped across the sky, ten strangers sought safety within the walls of the inn. Their fortunes were about to become **entwined** in a web of mystery and deception, **unbeknownst** to them.

Among the guests were Sneha, a troubled young woman haunted by her past, and Yash, a weary detective with a dark secret. As they arrived, they noticed the peculiar atmosphere that enveloped the inn. The guests included a renowned novelist, a married couple with a strained relationship, a suspicious doctor, a lost tourist, a reclusive artist, a mysterious woman, and an enigmatic priest.

They discovered the hotel's phone lines had gone dead, and the road outside had vanished into an endless abyss shortly after their arrival. Tensions rose as they realised they were being watched while trapped in the Desi Dhaba Hotel. Their terror grew as they discovered a series of disturbing photographs depicting their own deaths.

As the storm intensified, the guests began to doubt their identities and motives. Each carried secrets and the burden of guilt. As they suspected each other, trust deteriorated and paranoia set in. With no way out and no one to turn to, they were forced to solve the mystery that bound them together.

The guests died one by one, and gore and bloodshed covered the guest house, mirroring the fates depicted in the photographs. Desperate for survival, Sneha and Yash pieced together fragments of their shared past and the truth behind the enigmatic inn. They realised the hotel represented their deepest fears and guilt, a **purgatory** where they were forced to confront their sins.

As the sole survivor, Sneha was forced to confront her darkest secret—a tragic accident. In which she accidentally ran her car over a small girl on a stormy night, an incident that had haunted her for years. She discovered that the other visitors were all connected to her past, each representing a piece of her guilt and remorse. The inn had transformed into a twisted mirror, reflecting her own tortured soul.

Sneha and Yash raced against time to uncover the truth and escape the clutches of the Desi Dhaba Hotel in a heart-pounding climax. They discovered that facing their past and accepting their responsibility was the key to their freedom.

As the storm passed, the fog lifted, revealing Madhuban once more. Sneha and Yash emerged from the Hotel, their lives forever altered by their ordeal. Their lives would be intertwined forever, and the echoes of the Desi Dhaba Hotel would haunt them as a reminder of the darkness within.

"Fragments of Fate" is a psychological thriller that explores the depths of guilt, the fragility of identity, and the power of redemption. In the face of their own demons, the characters must confront their pasts and find the strength to escape the cycle of their own self-destruction.

WORD MEANINGS

1. **Entwined:** closely connected or unable to be separated
2. **Unbeknownst:** without a particular person knowing
3. **Purgatory:** the place to which Roman Catholics believe that the spirits of dead people go and suffer for the evil acts that they did while they were alive, before they are able to go to heaven

Chapter 4: "Case 37"

Aamishi, a compassionate social worker, once lived in a small town nestled among rolling hills. Aamishi, who is known for her dedication to protecting vulnerable children, was assigned a case that would put her resolve to the test and unravel her perception of reality.

Late one evening, Aamishi received a call from her supervisor, alerting her to a new case involving a young girl named Lily. Rumours circulated that Lily's parents were abusive, and her safety was at risk. Concerned for the child's well-being, Aamishi decided to visit the family's home that same night.

Aamishi felt uneasy as she approached the old, **dilapidated** house. The air was thick with an indescribable heaviness, and the darkness seemed to seep through its windows. Despite her reservations, she knocked on the door, determined to keep Lily safe.

Kabir and Preeti, Lily's parents, greeted Aamishi with forced smiles and hollow eyes. They denied any wrongdoing to their daughter and insisted that the accusations were unfounded. Aamishi couldn't shake the feeling that something was wrong, but she couldn't do anything without concrete evidence.

Days turned into weeks, and Aamishi couldn't shake the unsettling feeling that Lily was in danger. Nightmares plagued her sleep, vivid visions of a terrified young girl trapped in a nightmarish world. Determined to uncover the truth, Aamishi discreetly began her own investigation, digging into the family's history.

Her research uncovered a disturbing pattern of incidents surrounding Lily's parents. Mysterious deaths and disappearances seemed to follow them wherever they went. Aamishi's curiosity turned into an obsession as she delved deeper, unearthing a dark secret hidden within the town's forgotten history.

Aamishi continued her investigation and came across an underground cult with a sinister agenda. In exchange for power and immortality, the cult believed in sacrificing innocent children to summon supernatural entities. Lily's parents were not victims; they were cult members, and Lily was their planned sacrifice.

Aamishi's determination to save Lily grew stronger, but time was running out. She reached out to a local detective, Yash, sharing her findings and pleading for his assistance. Together, they formulated a plan to rescue Lily and bring down the cult once and for all.

Aamishi and Yash infiltrated the cult's secret meeting under cover of darkness, armed with evidence and a fierce determination to protect Lily. The cult members, clad in black robes, went about their twisted

rituals, oblivious to the impending confrontation.

In a climactic showdown, Aamishi and Yash fought against the cult's members, desperately trying to reach Lily. The air crackled with dark energy as the ritual neared its climax. Time seemed to slow as Aamishi faced the cult's leader, a **malevolent** figure shrouded in darkness.

Aamishi summoned every ounce of courage she could muster and confronted the cult leader, engaging in a battle of wills and strength. As the final moments approached, Aamishi's fortitude triumphed, and the dark forces were defeated.

In the aftermath, Lily was rescued and placed in the care of a loving foster family. Aamishi's relentless determination and unwavering belief in protecting the innocent had saved another life. Though scarred by the horrors she had witnessed, Aamishi found solace in the knowledge that she had made a difference.

As Aamishi reflected on her harrowing journey, she realised that evil could manifest in the most unexpected places. The boundaries between the real and the supernatural were thin, and it was the duty of those who dared to face the darkness to protect the innocent.

And so, Aamishi continued her work, forever vigilant, for she knew that evil could take on many forms, and the battle against it would never truly end.

WORD MEANINGS

1. **Dilapidated:** old and in poor condition.
2. **Malevolent:** causing or wanting to cause harm or evil.

Chapter 5 : "Fragile Innocence"

Once a bustling family, the Sharmas found themselves torn apart by a tragedy that shattered their lives. Seeking solace, they decided to adopt a child, hoping to rebuild their broken home. Little did they know that their innocent decision would plunge them into a nightmare they could never have imagined.

The Sharmas' journey began when they came across an orphanage nestled in the countryside. They were immediately drawn to Kriti, a young girl with an angelic face and sad eyes. Her delicate appearance masked a troubled past, but the Sharmas saw a chance to provide her with the love and stability she desperately needed.

When they brought Kriti home, they embraced her as their own, eager to show her the love she had been denied for so long. Their idyllic vision was quickly shattered when Kriti's behaviour became unsettling. Strange occurrences began to occur, leading the family to question their decision.

At first, it seemed like an innocent prank. Toys mysteriously moved, whispers echoed through the halls, and shadows danced in the corners of their eyes. The Sharmas dismissed these occurrences as mere coincidences, but deep down, they couldn't shake the feeling that something was amiss.

As time passed, Kriti's actions grew increasingly disturbing. Animals would go missing, only to be discovered strangely dead and cut into pieces in the backyard. The Sharmas discovered dark secrets hidden in Kriti's room—disturbing drawings and unsettling writings that hinted at a troubled psyche. Desperate for answers, they embarked on a journey to uncover Kriti's past, visiting the orphanage where she had spent her early years.

They discovered a terrifying truth there. Kriti was not the person she appeared to be. Aashi was her real name, and she had escaped from a notorious psychiatric institution. Aashi had a severe **dissociative identity disorder**, which allowed various personalities to emerge and take control.

The revelation terrified the Sharmas and trapped them in a psychological game. Aashi's true nature revealed itself, and she revelled in their terror. She expertly pitted each family member against each other, exploiting their flaws and vulnerabilities.

As the Sharmas fought to regain control of their lives, they realised that Aashi's malevolent presence extended far beyond their home. They found evidence of her involvement in previous tragedies, linking her to a string of mysterious deaths surrounding her past adoptive families.

In a race against time, the Sharmas sought the help of a renowned psychiatrist named Yash who specialised in dissociative disorders. Together, they devised a plan to confront Aashi and integrate her fractured personality, hoping to free her from the grip of darkness.

In a final, chilling confrontation, the Sharmas faced Aashi head-on, armed with love and determination. They discovered the source of Aashi's pain—a haunting childhood trauma that had fractured her mind. While her mother encouraged her to take piano lessons, young Aashi didn't enjoy the instrument. Her mother beat and tortured her after she erred, and one day, out of rage, she killed her mother. Through empathy and understanding, Yash and The Sharmas endeavoured to heal her wounded soul.

"Fragile Innocence" is a psychological thriller that delves into the complexities of identity, trauma, and the lengths a family will go to protect one another. It explores the darkest corners of the human psyche and challenges the boundaries of love and forgiveness in the face of unimaginable evil.

Chapter 6: "Abyss of Sanity"

Rahul Kapoor was a successful investment banker living in the heart of the city. With his impeccable style, charming demeanour, and enviable wealth, he seemed to have it all. But beneath the veneer of success, Rahul harboured a dark secret—a side of him that thrived on sadistic pleasures.

From the outside, Rahul appeared like any other respectable businessman, admired and respected by his peers. However, behind closed doors, he descended into a twisted world of violence and

depravity. His pristine penthouse became a chamber of horrors, hidden beneath a meticulously organised life.

Rahul's routine began **innocuously**, blending seamlessly with the hustle and bustle of the city. He attended business meetings, socialised with the elite, and indulged in the trappings of his lavish lifestyle. However, as night fell, he delved into his true obsession—a **macabre** game of power and control.

His victims were carefully chosen, typically young women drawn into his web of deceit. Rahul enjoyed the thrill of manipulation, toying with their emotions before plunging them into a nightmarish abyss. He revelled in their terror, deriving pleasure from their suffering.

He meticulously planned each encounter, ensuring that his true identity remained concealed. His mask of sanity held firmly in place, even as he lured innocent victims into his trap. He relished the power he held over their lives, savouring the perverse dance of dominance and submission.

As the body count rose, a detective named Yash became suspicious of the string of mysterious disappearances. Driven by an unwavering determination to uncover the truth, he began connecting the dots, drawing ever closer to Rahul's dark secret.

Rahul became increasingly reckless as he became more aware of the increasing **scrutiny**. His once ironclad control began to ebb, leaving a breadcrumb trail for Detective Yash to follow. The cat and mouse game between them became more intense, leading to a terrifying climax for both.

Rahul spiralled into insanity, caught between his growing desire for violence and the imminent threat of exposure. The lines between reality and fantasy became increasingly blurred, driving him deeper into the abyss of his own fractured mind.

Detective Yash cornered Rahul in his lair in a final confrontation. Rahul's sanity mask shattered as the truth was revealed, revealing the monster within. The ensuing conflict was a violent clash of wills, with each side determined to win.

In the end, the battle between good and evil reached its climax, leaving scars on both sides. Detective Yash emerged triumphant, having uncovered the true extent of Rahul's depravity. The horrors hidden behind his polished façade were exposed for the world to see.

"Abyss of Sanity" is a chilling exploration of the darkness that resides within seemingly ordinary individuals. It delves into the depths of the human psyche, questioning the nature of morality and the fragile boundaries of sanity. Prepare to confront the uncomfortable truth that evil can lurk behind the most charming of smiles.

WORD MEANINGS

1. **Depravity:** the state of being morally bad, or an action that is morally bad.

2. **Innocuously:** in a way that is completely harmless

3. **Macabre:** used to describe something that is very strange and unpleasant because it is connected with death or violence

4. **Scrutiny:** the careful and detailed examination of something in order to get information about it

Chapter 7 : "The Ultimatum Experiment"

It was a cold, stormy night when ten strangers gathered inside a windowless room, each one vying for a life-altering opportunity. They had been selected from a pool of highly qualified individuals, all hoping to secure a coveted position at a prestigious organisation. But little did they know that the path to success would be far more twisted and treacherous than they could ever imagine.

Dr. Pratyaksha Chopra, a renowned psychologist, stood at the front of the room. She had been hired by the organisation to oversee a unique and gruelling selection process. As the clock struck midnight, the tension in the room was palpable.

"Welcome," Dr. Chopra began, her voice echoing through the room. "You have all been chosen for an experiment that will test your abilities, resilience, and integrity. Only one of you will emerge victorious and earn the position you desire."

Confusion and curiosity filled the air as the participants exchanged wary glances. Dr. Chopra continued, "Inside this room, you will find a single question, but the answer is not as important as the path you take to find it. You have thirty minutes, and your only rule is this: do whatever it takes to succeed."

The room erupted with questions, but Dr. Chopra silenced them with a wave of her hand. She explained that hidden cameras would capture their every move, and their actions would be observed by the organisation's top executives. The participants understood that their decisions and behaviour would shape their fate.

The participants frantically searched the room as the timer began its relentless countdown. They looked everywhere for clues, including the walls, furniture, and even each other. As alliances formed and disbanded, secrets were revealed, and betrayals occurred, tensions rose.

Inside the room, there were no heroes or villains—only individuals desperate to win. As the clock dwindled, desperation fueled their actions. They resorted to manipulation, deception, and even sabotage to gain an advantage over their competitors.

One participant, Yash, took a different approach. He realised that the true test was not solely about the answer but about the manner in which it was obtained. He chose to resist the temptation to compromise his values and instead focused on building alliances and fostering cooperation among the group.

As time ticked away, Yash discovered a hidden compartment in the floor, containing a key. With just minutes remaining, he shared his finding with the group, urging them to work together to unlock the final puzzle.

The group's dynamics shifted as they realised that their best chance of success lay in collaboration. They pooled their knowledge and skills, piecing together fragments of information scattered throughout the room. As they worked together, they unravelled the mystery, unlocking a final box that revealed the answer to the question.

The room fell silent as Dr. Chopra announced the end of the experiment. The participants, still catching their breath, stared at each other, realising the lessons they had learned throughout the intense ordeal.

Dr. Chopra addressed them one last time. "Congratulations to all of you. The organisation has been observing your actions closely, not just during the competition but throughout your journey. Remember, success is not merely measured by the destination but by the integrity and collaboration you exhibit along the way."
The participants left the room, forever changed by the experience. Some emerged triumphant, securing their positions in the organisation. Others found solace in the newfound friendships and lessons learned. Regardless of the outcome, they all carried with them the indelible mark of "The Ultimatum Experiment," forever mindful of the choices they made and the value of integrity and cooperation in their pursuit of success.

Chapter 8 : "Eternal Shadows"

The wind howled through the desolate mountain pass, carrying with it an air of foreboding as Shaurya steered his car towards his new home for the winter—a grand, isolated mansion nestled deep within the snow-capped peaks. With his wife, Mona, and their young son, Jonty, by his side, Shaurya sought solace in this secluded retreat, taking on the role of caretaker during the off-season. Little did they know that their stay at the mountain lodge would unleash a chilling descent into madness.

Mr. Yash, the mansion's head caretaker, greeted the family upon their arrival, and his unsettling **demeanour** put Shaurya on edge. The Singhs felt increasingly isolated as the days turned into weeks. Shaurya, an aspiring writer, was suffering from writer's block, and Mona sensed an unsettling presence lurking in the shadows.

In the heart of the mansion lay the forbidden ballroom, its entrance guarded by a heavy door that whispered secrets from the past. As the days grew colder and the nights darker, Jonty, gifted with a supernatural ability known as "the gleaming," began to see glimpses of a haunting presence within the ballroom's reflective mirrors.

Shaurya's frustrations mounted, his mind spiralling into a dark abyss. The once-charming mansion transformed into a labyrinth of hallways, its walls seemingly closing in on him. The spirits of former guests whispered in his ears, fueling his descent into madness. Shadows danced before his eyes, luring him towards the forbidden ballroom.

Mona, consumed by her own fears, desperately sought a way to protect Jonty and escape the clutches of the mansion's sinister hold. As her own grip on reality wavered, she discovered a hidden library, its shelves lined with books chronicling the mansion's dark history.

Mona discovered the truth buried within the library's depths: the mansion had once been a place of unspeakable horrors, its walls soaked in the blood of victims caught in a cycle of violence and despair. It was a place that preyed on the living's vulnerability, drawing them deeper into its grasp.

With this newfound knowledge, Mona resolved to save her family. She searched for a way to break the mansion's malevolent power, seeking guidance from the spirits that lingered within its walls. They whispered cryptic messages, guiding her towards a final confrontation with the darkness that consumed the mansion.

Meanwhile, Shaurya's descent into madness reached its peak. He became possessed by the spirits of the past, their voices echoing through his mind, urging him to unleash his rage upon his own family. The ballroom's mirrors became portals to alternate dimensions, reflecting his fractured psyche.

Mona confronted Shaurya in a climactic showdown, her love for him battling the malevolent forces that possessed him. She fought to break the cycle of violence and free her family from the eternal shadows that engulfed the mansion, aided by the spirits of the mansion.

As the echoes of their struggle subsided, the mansion stood silent once more, its halls haunted by the ghosts of the past. Mona, Jonty, and the spirits of the victims found solace in their release from the mansion's grip. With the final flicker of a dying candle, they emerged from the depths of darkness into the dawn of a new beginning.

"Eternal Shadows" serves as a chilling reminder that some places hold an insidious power, preying on the vulnerabilities of the living. It is a tale of resilience and love, as one family fights against the forces of darkness to reclaim their sanity and find light amidst eternal shadows.

WORD MEANINGS

Demeanour: a way of looking and behaving

Chapter 9 : "Beyond the Veil"

Once upon a time in a quiet suburban neighbourhood, lived a peculiar young boy named Golu. At the tender age of seven, Golu had an extraordinary gift – the ability to see and communicate with spirits. However, he kept this secret locked away, for he feared the reactions of those around him.

Golu's life took a dramatic turn when his family moved into an old Victorian house with a haunting history. Unbeknownst to his parents, the house was once a gathering place for restless spirits trapped in limbo, desperately seeking closure.

Strange occurrences began to occur shortly after we arrived. Doors creaked open and shut by themselves, whispers echoed through the corridors, and chilling draughts chilled the air. Despite his fear, Golu felt a connection to these apparitions and heard their cry for help.

One evening, while exploring the attic, Golu discovered an old journal belonging to a previous owner of the house. The entries described a tragic event where a young girl named Riya had mysteriously disappeared without a trace. It became evident to Golu that the spirits he encountered were the lost souls of Riya and others who met a similar fate.

With the help of Dr. Yash, a renowned child psychologist who specialised in the paranormal, Golu mustered the courage to confide in her about his unique ability. Driven by empathy and a desire to set the spirits free, Golu and Dr. Yash embarked on a journey to uncover the truth behind the lingering hauntings.

Together, they delved into the house's dark history, discovering a web of secrets, betrayal, and unsolved mysteries. As Golu and Dr. Yash explored the past, they were confronted by vengeful spirits and confronted their own fears.

Meanwhile, Golu's parents grew increasingly concerned about their son's behaviour. They attributed his strange mannerisms and distant demeanour to a vivid imagination and sought conventional medical help. This strained their relationship and tested their understanding of their son's true nature.

As Golu's connection with the spirits deepened, he began to witness flashbacks and relive the final moments of their lives. He realised that their deaths were not mere accidents but intentional acts of violence. Uncovering the truth became paramount, not only to provide closure for the spirits but to bring justice to those responsible.

In a chilling climax, Golu and Dr. Yash confront the malicious entity responsible for orchestrating the tragic events in the house. Together, they unravelled a tale of greed, betrayal, and revenge, exposing the culprit and providing the spirits with the closure they so desperately sought.

Through their joint efforts, the house transformed from a place of fear and darkness into a sanctuary of peace. The spirits, finally finding solace, crossed over to the other side, leaving Golu with a newfound sense of purpose and a sense of closure for himself.

"Beyond the Veil" is a haunting tale of empathy, bravery, and the enduring power of the human spirit. It explores the realms of the supernatural, challenging the boundaries between the living and the dead while reminding us of the importance of compassion and understanding.

Chapter 10 : "The Fragmented Reflection"

The air in the dimly lit apartment was thick with tension as Abhi sat
alone, his gaze fixed upon the cracked mirror hanging on the wall. A
hollow, emaciated figure stared back at him, his haunted eyes
reflecting a deep-seated torment. Abhi's memory was fragmented, his
past obscured by a fog of confusion and self-doubt.

Months ago, he had found himself entangled in a bizarre accident,
resulting in the death of a mysterious woman. Since then, his mind
had become a twisted labyrinth of guilt and **paranoia**. Sleep eluded
him, leaving him perpetually fatigued and tormented by strange
visions.

Haunted by his actions, Abhi sought solace in his monotonous routine. He worked the night shift at a local factory, numbing his senses with endless repetition. Days blurred into nights, and reality became a **murky** haze. The few acquaintances he had left were wary of his presence, sensing the darkness that enveloped him.

In his quest for redemption, Abhi sought solace at a nearby support group. There, he met a fellow attendee named Sanwoyee, whose vibrant energy ignited a spark of hope within him. Sanwoyee, too, carried her own emotional burdens, and their shared pain drew them closer together.

As their friendship deepened, Sanwoyee revealed fragments of her own troubled past. She had been a victim of abuse, and her strength in overcoming her trauma inspired Abhi. He began to confide in her, sharing the haunting visions that plagued his every waking moment. Sanwoyee urged him to confront his inner demons, to unravel the mysteries of his fractured mind.

Driven by a desperate need for answers, Abhi embarked on a treacherous journey into the depths of his subconscious. Night after night, he delved into his dreams, hoping to uncover the truth that lay hidden within. But his fractured memories twisted and distorted, leading him further into a state of confusion.

As Abhi's grip on reality continued to loosen, he became convinced that he was being watched. Strange occurrences plagued his apartment—objects moved inexplicably, whispers echoed through the walls, and shadows danced in the corners of his vision. He suspected a malevolent presence lurking just beyond his perception.

Paranoia consumed him as he frantically searched for clues to the enigmatic woman's identity, visiting the places from his fragmented memories. The more he unravelled, the more he questioned his own sanity. Was he truly a victim, or was he an unwitting pawn in a larger game?

One night, Abhi's relentless pursuit brought him to a dilapidated warehouse—an eerie place filled with haunting echoes. There, he discovered a hidden room, adorned with photographs and newspaper clippings, connecting him to a past he couldn't fully remember. A chilling realisation struck him—his accident, the mysterious woman's death, and his fragmented memories were all part of a carefully constructed **façade**.

Driven to the brink of madness, Abhi confronted the true architect of his torment—a manipulative mastermind who had meticulously orchestrated his descent into darkness. The enigmatic figure revelled in his power over Abhi, exploiting his vulnerabilities and fragile state of mind.

In a desperate bid for **liberation**, Abhi fought back, rallying the last **vestiges** of his strength. He had become a shell of his former self, but within that broken shell lay the potential for rebirth. With Abhi's support, he embraced the truth, unravelling the tangled web of deception that had **ensnared** him.

As the final pieces of the puzzle fell into place, Abhi emerged from the depths of his despair. The fragmented mirror shattered, reflecting a man no longer haunted by his past. The path to redemption was **arduous**, but his journey through the fractured recesses of his mind had led him to an undeniable truth—he was not defined by his darkest moments, but rather by his capacity to heal and find redemption.

"The Fragmented Reflection" is a haunting tale of self-discovery, resilience, and the profound impact of the human psyche. It explores the depths of guilt, paranoia, and the search for identity amidst a fractured reality. Through Abhi's harrowing journey, we are reminded of the resilience of the human spirit and the potential for transformation, even in the face of unimaginable darkness.

WORD MEANINGS

1. **Paranoia:** an extreme and unreasonable feeling that other people do not like you or are going to harm or criticise you
In Psychology: Someone who has paranoia has unreasonable false beliefs as a part of another mental illness, for example **schizophrenia**.

2. **Schizophrenia:** a serious mental illness in which someone cannot understand what is real and what is imaginary

3. **Murky:** dark and dirty or difficult to see through.

4. **Façade:** the front of a building, especially a large or attractive building.

5. **Liberation:** an occasion when something or someone is released or made free.

6. **Vestiges:** a small part or amount of something larger, stronger, or more important that still exists from something that existed in the past.

7. **Ensnared:** to catch or get control of something or someone.

8. **Arduous:** difficult, needing a lot of effort and energy.

Chapter 11 : "Whispers of Redemption: The Search for Truth"

Once a bustling metropolis, the city had become a haunted shadow of its former glory. Among its dilapidated buildings and gloomy alleys, a dark secret thrived. Inspector Arjun Mehta, a seasoned investigator haunted by his own tragic past, found himself thrust into a mystifying case that would challenge everything he believed in.

Arjun had never believed in the supernatural, attributing it to mere superstition. However, when he was assigned to investigate a series of mysterious deaths linked to a dilapidated theatre, his scepticism was put to the test. Whispers of a ghostly woman, dressed in white, and her involvement in the accidents had spread throughout the city.

Haunted by guilt over his wife's untimely demise, Arjun was determined to uncover the truth behind the rumours and put the city's fears to rest. As he delved deeper into the case, he encountered a mysterious actress named Maya, who claimed to have a connection to the supernatural occurrences.

Together, Arjun and Maya embarked on a perilous journey, navigating through the city's underbelly and unearthing long-buried secrets. As they dug deeper, they uncovered a network of deceit and betrayal, where powerful individuals manipulated the truth for their own gain.

Arjun's relentless pursuit of the truth led him to confront his own demons and question his sanity. The lines between reality and illusion began to blur as he experienced unexplained encounters and eerie coincidences. With each step closer to the truth, Arjun found himself entangled in a web of lies that threatened to consume him.

As the pieces of the puzzle fell into place, Arjun discovered that the deaths were not mere accidents but a meticulously planned cover-up. The ghostly woman in white was a symbol of justice seeking retribution for the oppressed and the silenced.

Driven by a newfound purpose, Arjun vowed to expose the truth, regardless of the consequences. He risked his career, reputation, and even his life to bring the hidden truths to light. Along the way, he learned the power of redemption and the importance of facing one's past.

In a heart-stopping climax, Arjun confronted the mastermind behind the theatre's secrets, unmasking the true identity of the woman in white. The city, once trapped in the grip of fear and deceit, found solace in the unravelling of the truth.

"Whispers of Redemption" is a haunting tale that explores the depths of guilt, redemption, and the human desire for truth. Through a captivating narrative, it reminds us that answers lie within our own souls, waiting to be unearthed, and that sometimes, the search for truth leads to unexpected self-discovery.

Chapter 12 : "Fractured Identity: A Journey Within"

It was a monotonous existence for Raj, a mild-mannered office worker trapped in the suffocating grip of a mundane life. Every day, he followed the same routine, devoid of purpose or excitement. Raj longed for something more, something that would ignite a spark within him and shake him out of his soul-numbing routine.

One evening, while surfing the internet, Raj stumbled upon an underground community known as "The Fragmented Minds." This secretive group promised a radical transformation, a liberation from the chains of conformity. Intrigued, Raj attended one of their clandestine meetings held in an abandoned warehouse.

The meeting room was dimly lit, filled with people wearing dark clothes and masks. The charismatic leader, known as The Architect, addressed the crowd, speaking passionately about the power of chaos and the necessity of breaking free from societal constraints. Raj's curiosity piqued as The Architect revealed a radical philosophy centred around embracing one's true desires and unleashing repressed emotions.

Over time, Raj grew enamoured with The Fragmented Minds, forming a bond with his fellow members who yearned for a sense of purpose and liberation. Inspired by their rebellious spirit, Raj adopted a new identity, calling himself "Alex"." He started to attend underground boxing matches organised by the group, where participants fought not only physically but also to redefine themselves.

Under the guidance of The Architect and the **tutelage** of an enigmatic figure known as The Sid, Alex embarked on a transformational journey, delving into the depths of his psyche. He underwent intense physical training, seeking to conquer his own limitations and unlock the dormant potential within.

But as Alex immersed himself deeper into this **clandestine** world, the line between reality and illusion began to blur. He started experiencing vivid hallucinations and gaps in his memory, unable to distinguish between his alter ego and his true self. The concept of identity became a fragile construct, with Alex losing his grip on who he truly was.

Meanwhile, The Fragmented Minds began executing audacious acts of societal disruption, targeting symbols of consumerism and conformity. Alex found himself torn between the seductive allure of chaos and the moral implications of their actions. The consequences of their activities started to unravel around him, leading to violence and chaos that mirrored the **turmoil** within his own mind.

In a climactic twist, Alex discovered that both The Architect and The Sid were manifestations of his own fractured psyche. They were personifications of his desires and fears, serving as catalysts for his journey of self-discovery. The battles he fought in the boxing ring mirrored the internal struggle to reconcile his fragmented identities.

As the truth unravelled, Alex confronted the shattered pieces of his own psyche. He realised that true liberation lay not in external rebellion, but in embracing his own flaws and accepting the complexity of his identity. With this newfound understanding, Alex chose to dismantle The Fragmented Minds, recognizing that true change begins from within.

"Fractured Identity: A Journey Within" is a gripping exploration of the human psyche, blending themes of self-discovery, rebellion, and the consequences of losing touch with reality. It challenges readers to question the nature of identity and the importance of embracing the complexities that make us who we are.

WORD MEANINGS

1. **Tutelage:** help, advice, or teaching about how to do something.

2. **Clandestine:** planned or done in secret, especially describing something that is not officially allowed

3. **Turmoil:** a state of confusion, uncertainty, or disorder

Chapter 13 : "City of Shadows"

It was a rainy night in the heart of the city. The neon lights flickered against the dark backdrop, casting an eerie glow on the deserted streets. Lakshay, a **disillusioned** war veteran in his mid-thirties, found himself driving through the labyrinthine streets of this urban jungle. Haunted by his past experiences, he sought solace in the darkness that enveloped the city.

Lakshay's life had become a monotonous routine of driving his taxi through the city's streets, observing the filth and decadence that seemed to thrive in every corner. The rich flaunted their wealth while the destitute fought for scraps, and he was an unwilling witness to it all.

One fateful evening, a woman named Ayesha entered Lakshay's cab. She exuded an air of vulnerability that stirred something deep within him. Her soft-spoken voice and haunted eyes resonated with the pain he had buried inside himself. They struck up a conversation, and Lakshay felt an unexplainable connection to her.

Over time, Lakshay and Ayesha developed a friendship that grew stronger with each passing night. They found solace in their shared experiences of isolation and disillusionment. Ayesha revealed that she was a struggling actress, desperate to escape the clutches of a manipulative and abusive manager named Yash.

Driven by his growing affection for Ayesha, Lakshay made it his mission to liberate her from Yash's clutches. The city had become a **cesspool** of corruption, and Lakshay was determined to become its unlikely vigilante. He trained rigorously, honing his combat skills and acquiring an arsenal of weapons.

As he ventured deeper into the underbelly of the city, Lakshay encountered a network of criminals, drug dealers, and pimps. He waged a one-man war against them, using his knowledge of the city's darkest secrets to his advantage. Lakshay became a symbol of fear among the wicked, striking fear into the hearts of those who preyed on the innocent.

However, as Lakshay's actions grew increasingly violent, his own sanity began to unravel. The lines between justice and vengeance blurred, and he found himself descending into a twisted world of moral **ambiguity**. The city had infected his soul, turning him into a monster he had sworn to destroy.

Lakshay's relentless pursuit of justice led him to Yash's lair—a dilapidated warehouse on the outskirts of town. In a climactic confrontation, Lakshay confronted Yash and his henchmen. The battle was fierce and brutal, a manifestation of the demons that had plagued Lakshay for far too long. Ayesha, however, intervened in the fight at that precise moment and was brutally murdered in front of Lakshay.

In the end, Lakshay emerged victorious, his body battered and his mind scarred. He had rid the city of one of its vilest parasites, but at a tremendous cost to his own humanity and love. The rain continued to pour as Lakshay stood amidst the ruins of his self-imposed war.

As the sirens wailed in the distance, Lakshay realised that the city would continue to be consumed and corrupt, no matter how many battles he fought. He couldn't save everyone, nor could he save himself. The city had become his eternal purgatory, and he was destined to roam its shadowy streets, forever haunted by the ghosts of his own past.

And so, Lakshay returned to his taxi, a silent guardian navigating the twisted roads of the city. He became one with the darkness, forever tormented by the relentless beat of the city's heart. In this urban jungle, he was just another shadow, lost amidst the chaos and despair that defined "City of Shadows."

WORD MEANINGS

1. **Disillusioned:** disappointed and unhappy because of discovering the truth about something or someone that you liked or respected.

2. **Cesspool:** a large underground hole or container that is used for collecting and storing solid waste, urine, and dirty water.

3. **Ambiguity:** the fact of something having more than one possible meaning and therefore possibly causing confusion

Chapter 14 : "Whispers of Darkness"

It was a cold, dreary evening as Agent Monika stepped into the grim confines of the Agra State Penitentiary. She had been assigned to interview one of the most notorious criminals of their time, Dr.Yash, a brilliant psychiatrist turned psychopath. The FBI sought his assistance in capturing a sadistic serial killer, known as The Rakshasa, who had been terrorising the city for months.

Yash, now confined in a high-security cell, exuded an eerie aura. Dressed in a crisp white shirt and meticulously combed silver hair, he seemed out of place in the dimly lit interrogation room. Monika had heard whispers of Yash's ability to manipulate and control others, and she knew she had to tread carefully.

Their first meeting was chilling. Yash studied her with penetrating eyes, his gaze seemingly peering into her very soul. He agreed to help, but with one chilling condition—he would only share his knowledge if Monika delved into her own dark past and confronted her deepest fears.

Reluctantly, Monika began her descent into the twisted world of her memories. She revisited her childhood home, where a tragic incident had occurred, leaving scars on her psyche. With each visit, the boundaries between reality and nightmare blurred, and Monika questioned her own sanity.

As Monika delved deeper into her past, The Rakshasa's killings intensified, leaving the city in a state of fear. The killer seemed to possess an uncanny ability to change his appearance, making him nearly impossible to identify. Monika grew desperate, turning to Yash for guidance, unsure if she could trust him or if he was merely manipulating her fragile psyche.

Under Yash's guidance, Monika's memories unveiled shocking revelations, connecting her tragic past to the present case. She realised that The Rakshasa had been silently watching her all along, exploiting her vulnerabilities. The line between hunter and hunted blurred, and Monika found herself caught in a dangerous game of cat and mouse.

As the climax approached, Monika uncovered The Rakshasa's hideout—a secluded, decaying mansion buried deep within the woods. With trepidation, she ventured inside, armed with the knowledge Yash had bestowed upon her. It was there that she confronted The Rakshasa, a twisted individual with an insatiable thirst for control and power.

In a nerve-racking showdown, Monika utilised her newfound strength to outwit and capture The Rakshasa. But the victory came at a great cost, as she grappled with the horrors of her past and the darkness that lay within her own soul.

As the story concluded, Monika emerged as a changed person, forever scarred but determined to confront her demons head-on. The chilling whispers of Dr. Yash would linger in her mind, a constant reminder of the darkness that resided within humanity.

A few weeks after the Rakshasa's capture, mysteriously, Dr. Yash broke out of the prison and is now roaming the streets of Agra at will. She developed a strange feeling that Dr. Yash is after her and will eventually kill her after learning about Dr. Yash's escape. Monika experienced severe anxiety as a result of believing that a psychopath was after her, and she continues to experience hauntings.

"Whispers of Darkness" is a psychological thriller that delves into the depths of the human psyche, exploring the fine line between good and evil, sanity and madness. It captivates readers with its twisted plot, intricate characters, and haunting revelations, leaving them questioning their own perception of reality.

Chapter 15 : "Shattered Reflections"

Once a thriving city filled with hope, Noida had fallen into despair and corruption. In the heart of its darkest alleys lived Vikram, a troubled and isolated man, yearning for recognition and purpose in a society that had forgotten him.

Vikram, haunted by a traumatic childhood and burdened by mental illness, struggled to make ends meet as a failed actor . Society's relentless indifference pushed him to the fringes of sanity, his laughter a mere facade masking his deep-seated pain.

One fateful day, Vikram's life took an unexpected turn when he stumbled upon a disturbing secret. Deep within the city's underbelly, he discovered evidence of a vast conspiracy, orchestrated by the wealthy elite, that exploited the vulnerable for their own gain.

Driven by a newfound purpose and a desire for justice, Vikram took on the persona of "The Daanav," a symbol of chaos and rebellion against the oppressive forces of Noida. With his face hidden behind a grotesque mask, he embarked on a mission to expose the truth, wielding his newfound power to strike fear into the hearts of the corrupt.

As "The Daanav," Vikram's acts of vigilantism garnered attention from both the oppressed and the powerful. The city became divided, torn between those who saw him as a symbol of hope and those who feared his unpredictable nature.

But as Vikram's vendetta escalated, the line between hero and villain blurred. The chaos he unleashed threatened to consume him entirely, his fractured psyche descending into a maelstrom of violence and madness. The more he tried to resist the darkness, the more it seduced him, eroding his sanity and fueling his uncontrollable laughter.

As Noida teetered on the edge of anarchy, Vikram's true identity was unveiled, exposing his vulnerability to the very forces he sought to dismantle. The powerful figures he had dared to challenge united against him, using their influence to manipulate public opinion and turn the city against him.

Isolated and cornered, Vikram found solace in the chaos, embracing the role of the villain he had inadvertently become. With each calculated act of violence, he sent shockwaves through the city, leaving a trail of broken dreams and shattered illusions in his wake.

In a final act of defiance, Vikram targeted the root of the conspiracy, a symbol of power and corruption. As he confronted the embodiment of everything he despised, a harrowing truth dawned upon him—the system was far greater than any individual. The city itself had become the ultimate antagonist, perpetuating a cycle of despair and broken souls.

In a climactic showdown, Vikram faced his demons head-on, both internal and external. In a blaze of chaos and desperation, he challenged the very essence of Noida, sacrificing himself to expose its festering wounds.

As the city grappled with the aftermath of Vikram's legacy, Noida was forced to confront its own reflection. The Ravana had become a symbol, a haunting reminder of the price of indifference and the consequences of societal neglect.

"Shattered Reflections" is a dark tale of a man's descent into madness, fueled by a broken society and his own inner demons. It explores the blurred boundaries between heroism and villainy, challenging readers to question the responsibility of individuals and the collective in the creation of a fractured world.

Chapter 16 : "Hidden Reflections"

Once a celebrated author, Siddharth now lives a reclusive life in a remote cabin tucked away in the heart of a dense forest. Haunted by his past success and tormented by writer's block, he spends his days immersed in solitude, desperately seeking inspiration. Little does he know that an unexpected visitor is about to unravel his world.

One stormy evening, a mysterious man named Yash arrives at Siddharth's cabin, claiming that Siddharth's latest bestselling novel was plagiarised from his own work. Siddharth vehemently denies the accusation, dismissing Yash as delusional. However, as Yash's threats escalate and evidence mounts against him, Siddharth finds himself questioning his own memory and sanity.

As the days pass, strange occurrences unfold around Siddharth. Pages from his manuscript go missing, eerie messages are scrawled on his walls, and unsettling photographs appear on his doorstep. Convinced that Yash is behind these disturbing events, Siddharth begins to unravel the truth about his alleged plagiarism and Yash's relentless pursuit.

In his desperate search for answers, Siddharth digs deeper into his past and discovers long-forgotten secrets. Dark memories resurface, blurring the lines between reality and fiction. Haunted by guilt and paranoia, Siddharth's grip on sanity starts to slip.

Unable to trust anyone, Siddharth retreats further into seclusion, desperate to find evidence that will exonerate him. The isolation takes a toll on his mental state as he becomes consumed by a relentless obsession to prove his innocence. The boundaries between his novel and his reality blur, and he questions if he is living inside a story or if the story is consuming him.

As Siddharth inches closer to the truth, he realises that Yash is not just an ordinary man seeking justice. Yash represents a suppressed part of Siddharth's own psyche, a manifestation of his dark impulses and buried secrets. The battle between Siddharth and Yash intensifies, both vying for control over the shattered remnants of Siddharth's mind.

In a climactic showdown, Siddharth confronts his inner demons and confronts the truth about his past. The lines between protagonist and antagonist blur, leaving Siddharth questioning his own identity and the nature of reality itself. The revelation is both shocking and liberating, forcing Siddharth to face the consequences of his actions and decide his ultimate fate.

"Hidden Reflections" is a psychological thriller that explores the depths of guilt, identity, and the blurred boundaries between fiction and reality. It delves into the darkest corners of the human mind, revealing the fragility of perception and the haunting power of buried secrets.

THANKS FOR READING MY FIRST BOOK (VEIL OF PERCEPTION)

FOLLOW ME ON INSTAGRAM FOR REGULAR UPDATES : @emperorjha200
SUBSCRIBE TO MY YOUTUBE CHANNELS : APUN KA LIFESTYLE (LIFESTYLE)
The Cineman (Movie Review)

MY OTHER WORKS :

A KID WITH A MILLION DREAMS AND CONNECTED THRU THE INTERNET ARE MY AUDIOBOOKS
AVAILABLE ON AUDIO PLATFORMS ONLY IN HINDI :

SPOTIFY
AMAZON MUSIC
AUDIBLE
HUBHOPPER
GAANA
GOOGLE PODCASTS
JIO SAAVN
HUNGAMA
HTTPS://akidwithamilliondr.wixsite.com/my-site